The Small bun

Retold by Martin Waddell

Illustrated by T.S. Spookytooth

Collins

A hungry man baked a small bun.
He sat down with his wife to eat
the small bun but ...

… the small bun hopped off the dish and ran.
Its little legs ran so fast that the bun got away.

The small bun met a hungry sheep by the gate. "Lunch! Yummy-yum!" said the sheep.

"I am too fast for the man and his wife, and
I am too fast for you!" said the bun.
Its little legs ran so fast that the bun got away.

The small bun met a hungry goat in the lane.
"Stand still till I eat you!" said the goat.

6

"I am too fast for the man and his wife and the sheep, and I am too fast for you!" said the bun. Its little legs ran so fast that the bun got away.

The small bun met a cunning fox by the river. "What a plump little bun!" said the cunning fox, licking his lips.

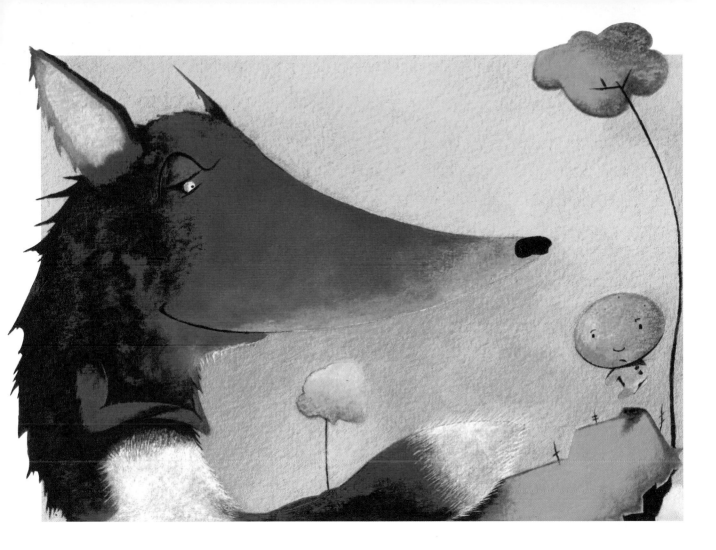

"I am too fast for the man and his wife, and the sheep, and the goat, and I am too fast for you!" said the bun.

But ...

… the river was there.
The small bun was trapped!
It kept running about, with the fox
running after it.
They ran so fast that they ran out of
running and stopped.

"You have beaten me," the fox huffed and puffed.
"Get on my back and I will carry you across
the river."

"If I get on your back, you will
eat me!" said the bun.
"Trust me," said the cunning fox.

The bun got on the back of the fox.
But the fox stopped in the middle of the river.
"Why have you stopped?" asked the bun.

"To eat you!" said the fox.
Gulp! Yum yum yum!
And that was the end of the bun.

A story map